75¢

Illustrations by LEONARD WEISGARD

ADAM and the
Golden Cock

by ALICE DALGLIESH

CHARLES SCRIBNER'S SONS *New York*

PRINTED IN THE UNITED STATES OF AMERICA

SBN 684-12438-6

Library of Congress Catalog Card Number 59-7206

AUTHOR'S NOTE

THIS story takes place in 1781 in Newtown, Connecticut. The main part of the story is true, though Adam and his family are imaginary. The golden cock is still on the steeple of a church in Newtown.

In July 1780, while the war of the American Revolution was being fought, General Rochambeau and his troops were sent from France to help. The general and his troops landed in Rhode Island. On their march from Rhode Island to the Hudson River, they stayed three days in Newtown. Washington might have met Rochambeau there, but his plans changed, and he asked the French general to bring his troops to the Hudson River without delay. From there the troops went on, all the way to Yorktown in Virginia and to victory.

We know a good deal about the march, and about Rochambeau's army, from records and maps made at the time. We know, from the writings of the French especially, a great deal about what Americans thought about the French, and what the French thought about the Americans. The help that the French gave to the

American army was of the greatest importance. At this time, Washington said that if the French did not come, "We are at the end of our tether." Not all of us remember that at this time the American army could not pay its soldiers, could not even feed them properly. When Rochambeau met Washington he gave the American general half of his "war chest"—twenty thousand dollars. This was generous, as Rochambeau did not know when the next money would come from France.

ADAM and the
Golden Cock

To the Weisgard children

ABIGAIL, CHRISTINA, and ETHAN

who often see the Golden Cock

CHAPTER I
ADAM AND THE GOLDEN COCK

Adam looked up at the golden cock on the church steeple.

"Tell me," he said, "will the soldiers come today? Will they march up the hill?"

Adam and the cock were friends. The boy knew it if the cock didn't. After all, the cock lived high in the air and he was covered with gold. Not gilt, but real gold. Nothing less.

Every morning Adam looked up at the cock. Did he swing to the north, to the south, to the east or to the west? The way the wind was blowing told something about the weather.

Weather was important when you had to be out in the pasture with the sheep. And in the many months when school did not keep, Adam helped the old shepherd with the town flock.

The golden cock looked small against the sky—but if Adam and the cock had been standing together on the ground the cock would have been the taller. And if the cock had been on the ground, Adam would have seen the bullet holes in him. There was one even in his proud, gold tail feathers.

Soldiers had fired those bullets—perhaps the British who were fighting George Washington. Soldiers, when they are not fighting and time goes slowly, can do a lot of things.

Adam had got into the way of talking to the cock because he was alone so much.

There were days when the old shepherd had to stay home because of his aching bones. Then Adam was alone, except for the sheep—and they were poor company. Silly things—they looked so much alike that you couldn't tell one from another, except for their owner's mark. One man's sheep had a halfpenny fastened on the under side of an ear. Other sheep had a nick in the left ear, or a nick in the right—and so it went.

The days were like the sheep—you could scarcely tell them apart. Often it seemed that nothing happened in a quiet little place like Newtown. Nothing.

And so Adam talked to the cock. After a time it seemed as if the cock answered him—not out loud of course, because that would have been plain queer. But the answer was there just the same, in Adam's

12 mind. To the question he'd asked there did not seem to be any answer,

WILL THE SOLDIERS COME TODAY?

This *was* a day when exciting things might happen. The old shepherd was at home, and there were Adam and the sheep

stuck in the pasture. He couldn't even go 13
to the top of the hill to see the soldiers
come marching into town.

These were special soldiers. They were
General Rochambeau's army, and they had
come all the way from France to fight with
the American army. People said that perhaps they were going to meet General

Washington right here in Newtown. All that happening and Adam could not go to see!

Was that music? Adam could not stand it any longer. All the people would be there—watching. What in the world were French soldiers like? Some said they were funny little men who painted their faces and curled their hair. Adam did not believe it---but he *had* to see. He had to see the general—Papa Rochambeau, as the soldiers called him. What could he do?

The music was coming nearer . . . nearer . . . nearer. Adam jumped to his feet. He would *have* to go. But the old shepherd had told him not to leave the sheep. Adam sat down again.

"Adam?"

The voice was right beside him, so close that Adam was startled. There stood his

friend Paul—at least Paul *had* been his
friend. Some time ago his father had told
him to keep away from Paul, not even to
speak to him. Paul's father was a Tory—
he was on the side of the King of England.
And Adam's father was in General Washington's army.

"Adam?"

Paul stood there waiting. Adam swallow-
ed and said nothing.

"Adam?"

He couldn't stand the question in Paul's voice. Perhaps it would be all right to *listen* if not to talk.

"Adam? They have told you not to speak to me because my father is a Loyalist. But you do not have to speak, just listen and shake your head—or nod."

The music was nearer. Papa Rochambeau's soldiers were coming!

Now Paul's words came with a rush.

"You want to see the soldiers? Then go —and I will stay with the sheep. No one wants *me* to see the soldiers. Go!"

Could he go? Adam waited a minute and thought. Should he leave the sheep with a boy whose father was a Tory? Paul wouldn't do anything wrong. . . . He couldn't hurt the sheep. Maybe he wouldn't stay with them, though.

"Adam?"

The music was a bold, swinging march. The soldiers must be coming up the hill. . . .

It was too much to stand. So he looked at Paul, nodded his head—and was off.

Paul picked up the shepherd's stick Adam had dropped, and sat down on a rock.

"They don't want me," he thought. "No one wants me because my father . . ."

The music was coming nearer, but it was not music for Paul.

CHAPTER II
MARCH, PAPA ROCHAMBEAU!

At the top of the long, steep hill Adam joined the crowd. His sister Abigail was there—he wondered if she would notice that he had left the sheep. But Abby was fifteen—and all aflutter over the soldiers. She did not even see Adam.

The French soldiers were not yet in sight. It was a hot day and they must be tired.

There was only the sound of music—such *different* music; such wonderful music. Adam made up words to it in his head:

March Papa Rochambeau, march,
March Papa Rochambeau,
March.

It was hard to wait. Adam looked up at his friend on the church steeple. The cock seemed to be watching and waiting, too.

Now the music was very near. Adam beat time to it with his foot.

March Papa Rochambeau,
March.

Here they came!

The sunlight glittered on the bayonets as the men marched up the hill. You couldn't see the men at first, just the tips of the bayonets, but they were coming.

And suddenly something inside Adam, something he had been trying not to listen to, told him he should not be there. The old shepherd had trusted him—and he had left the sheep with a Tory boy. To be with the sheep was Adam's job; he should not hand it over to anyone.

So, as the first soldiers came to the top of the hill, Adam did not see them. He had left the crowd and was running as fast as he could toward the pasture.

Abigail saw the running figure and wondered a little. The boy looked like her brother, but Adam was over in the pasture. He was a boy to be trusted even if he was a tease and a nuisance at times. He would *never* leave the sheep. And then Abigail forgot all about Adam, as the soldiers in their fine uniforms came marching up the hill. She stood on tiptoe to see them come.

Oh! they were wonderful! Red faced and
hot and tired—but those handsome white
uniforms . . . trimmed with black. . . . And
the drummers in their red, white and blue.
. . . The musicians in their white uniforms
trimmed with gold and silver braid. . . .
That man on the horse must be General
Rochambeau himself. . . . How Adam
would have loved to be here!

CHAPTER III
THEY ARE COMING HERE!

When Adam got back to the pasture Paul was gone. The old shepherd was sitting on the rock as if he had always been there.

"So," he said. "You left the sheep with Paul and went running off to see those French soldiers?"

"But I did not see them—I had to come back."

"That makes no difference. You should not have gone. Paul is a good boy, even if his father . . . but you should not have gone. I left the sheep in your care."

Adam wriggled. "I should not have gone. But the music . . . and the soldiers. . . . I wanted to see them."

"You are like all the rest. A fine uniform and you're off. Some day you will know that war is not all uniforms and flags and music. War is weariness—and sorrow —and death."

"I know all that," Adam said, annoyed that the old man seemed to think him stupid. "I know from my father that our soldiers are often hungry and cold. But he says we have no choice but to fight."

"Because we fight for our freedom. . . ." 23

The old shepherd was going on with his sermon endlessly—or so it seemed. For now the music was louder, it was coming nearer. . . .

"They are coming!" Adam shouted. "They are coming *here*!"

"Naturally," the old shepherd said. "And *here* is where you will get the best sight of them. For this is where they will camp."

"By Paul's house? Don't they know Paul's father is a Tory?"

The old shepherd smiled. "One Tory more or less makes little difference. They are all around—and some have even been friendly to the French. The soldiers will have been well warned."

Now both Adam and the old man forgot what they were talking about, forgot everything but the soldiers. They were not little

men with painted faces and curled hair.
They were real soldiers, in handsome uniforms. Adam could not have imagined
soldiers being dressed all in white—but
there they were—right before his eyes.
Their collars and lapels and cuffs were black,
but the uniforms were white. And those
red, white and blue drummers with their
copper drums!

They came ahead of supply wagons that
would bring their tents to be set up on the
camping ground. All that day they came.
The wagons began coming, too, drawn by
hot and tired oxen. It was hard for the
wagons to get into the camping ground for
there were big stones everywhere. One of
the wagons, so it was said, was full of silver coins.

"Though what they want of silver coins
is beyond me," the old shepherd said.

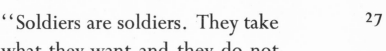

"Soldiers are soldiers. They take
what they want and they do not
pay for it. You will see."

CHAPTER IV
A SOLDIER NAMED PIERRE

If the first day was wonderful, the second was more so. Now that the tents were set up, the children gathered round to watch the soldiers. They couldn't talk to them, but they smiled and the soldiers smiled 28 back.

Adam was there, and some of the other
boys. Paul and his older brothers came
quietly across the field to see—and no one
said a word to them.

One young soldier—his name was Pierre
—seemed to gather all the children around
him, for he was always ready to answer
questions. And—to the great delight of the
children—he spoke English.

"You speak American well," Paul said. "How does it happen?"

"I speak English because my mother was English," Pierre said.

"Then why do you come to fight the English?"

Pierre thought a minute. Before he left France his mother had asked him the same question.

"One of our generals has told us this: 'We come not from hatred of the English but for love of liberty.'"

The children listened while Pierre told them many things. He told how Papa Rochambeau had brought almost everything from France that they would need to use. They had even brought bricks to build ovens to bake their bread.

"'The Americans have been fighting and they need all they have,' he said to us."

" 'Do not take a cabbage or a carrot that belongs to them. If we need what the people have, then we should pay for all we take.' "

"Is that what the silver coins are for?" Paul asked. The boys turned to look at him as if he had no right to ask a question. But Pierre answered him.

"Of course. Even the Indians who came to visit us when we were in Rhode Island were surprised that we did not take things. Branches with apples were hanging over our tents and we had not picked any."

Paul had come creeping quietly up until he stood near the French soldier. The boys stared at him as if he had no right to be there. They stared at him until he turned and walked away. His brothers followed.

Pierre looked down into the grass around the rock on which he was sitting. There were a few small strawberries. "After all these were wild ones. . . ."

He picked a ripe, red berry and ate it. "They grew in the fields around our farmhouse—over there in the South of France," he said. He ate another warm, red strawberry. "General Washington has told us, *Beware of country people bringing fruit. They may be spies.*"

He got up and walked away. Adam started across the fields to his house, thinking, "All soldiers must long to see their homes again. French soldiers are no different. . . . I wish I could see Papa Rochambeau." For the general stayed at his headquarters in the little town, and Adam longed to see him riding his horse, looking like a real general.

As Adam went past Paul's house, he was out in the field, picking wild strawberries.

34   Adam stopped. *What was Paul doing?*
What had Pierre said? Beware of country people
bringing fruit.

"Paul!" he said sharply. "What are you
doing? Why are you picking strawberries?"

Paul looked up, surprised that Adam was
speaking to him.

"I am picking strawberries because I
like to eat them." He looked straight at
Adam. "I do like strawberries—*you* know
that."

Adam knew it. Many times he and Paul
had picked strawberries together—here in
this meadow. He could not think of anything to say. He couldn't just say, "Are
you taking them to the French soldiers?
Will you try to find out their plans?"

So he walked on. Once or twice he
looked back. Paul was still picking strawberries.

CHAPTER V
THE GOLDEN COCK, AGAIN

March, march, march — a second regiment was coming to join the first! Pierre had told Adam the Royal Deux Ponts were coming. They were different from the Bourbonnais — Pierre's regiment — their breeches were white, but their coats were of a royal blue. All the Royal regiments wore blue coats, so Pierre said. Together the two regiments would form a brigade.

Adam would have liked to stop and watch them longer, but it was time for supper. Besides he had other things on his mind—things of importance. *Paul—strawberries—Beware of country people bringing fruit.*

General Washington might be here soon —he would *have* to see him. *Suppose . . . suppose General Washington didn't come?*

At supper Abigail was chattering, as always.

"Those French soldiers are so handsome! But how strange! We offered some of them tea, but they would not take it.

" 'You American ladies!' they said. 'Always drinking tea out of little china cups. It spoils your teeth!' And they say we do not know how to make bread. They like their French bread better, imagine! But they are polite, and say our bread is probably better for us."

Abigail paused for breath and Adam bit into his bread fiercely. Of course it was better than French bread.

"But they have white flour, so I hear," their mother said. "We have not had that

for some time. And your father has no
bread, no meat, sometimes no food for
days. The French have hard money, too,
and it is a long time since your father has
been paid."

"General Washington will see that he is
paid." Adam was loyal to his hero.

"Perhaps," his mother said. "Perhaps."

Abigail, seeing a break in the conversation, rushed in. "There is a soldier called
Pierre. He was here in the village earlier in
the day. He taught me some French words.
'People who can't understand each other
do not get on well together,' he said."

"What did he teach you?" Adam asked
without any real curiosity.

"*Bon jour*, Good morning. *Bon soir*, Good-
night. Such funny names they have for
things! Do you know what he calls strawberries? *Les fraises*. Imagine! *Les fraises*, the

strawberries. Oh, he is such a nice young man. I wish he did not have to go away.''

"He does not have to go until General Washington comes,'' said Adam.

"But I think he does. People are saying there has been a message . . . they say the general may not come. It's all very secret. And Pierre *did* have to go back to camp...."

Adam nearly choked. *Very secret*. The French soldiers might be changing their plans. Suppose Paul's father had sent him to find out?

The meal was over. Slowly Adam went upstairs to bed. From his small window he could see the golden cock. He stood by the window looking up at the cock, dark against the darker sky.

The thoughts went round and round in Adam's head. What should he do? How could he know? He tried to keep his

thoughts in order, but they kept stepping
out of line, tripping him up, confusing him.
It is difficult to make thoughts behave like
a regiment of well-drilled soldiers. No
matter what one does, some of those in the
back line *will* step forward.

What shall I do? Shall I tell someone?
If only Pa was here. Shall I tell my mother?

*No, it would frighten her and Pa told me to
take care of her.* Then anger came like a hot
flame. Paul is a spy. I *know* he is. *No, you
don't. And if you make a mistake. . . .*

But I saw him with the strawberries. I'd
like to sneak up behind him and hit him a
good one.

Then, one of those thoughts that do not
stay in line:

*The day I cut my foot in the pasture, Paul
helped me home.*

But . . .

And there was the time he . . .

Adam was being firm with his thoughts now. Oh, yes, Paul was his friend, but there was General Washington's army—and the French soldiers—Papa Rochambeau . . . his father. . . .

Now his eyes were almost closing. Thoughts could no longer keep him awake. He turned, unwillingly, and fell into bed without even time to get his head straight on the pillow. A lock of hair fell into his eyes but it didn't awaken him.

Then—the night was still dark—the golden cock was suddenly standing by Adam's bed. How enormous he was! From his golden feathers shone a pale yellow light.

44   Somehow it did not seem at all strange to have him standing there.

"Golden cock," said Adam. "Whatever would *you* do?"

"About what?" (Was the cock really speaking?)

"About Paul. He could be a spy." Adam explained it all, clearly and carefully. The cock listened, looking wise.

"Tell me," Adam said. "What shall I *do*?"

The cock turned slowly on its one slender leg and the light from the golden feathers seemed to fill the room.

"I tell–only–the–way–the–wind–blows," said the cock. "You must decide for yourself what is right. I–tell–only–the–way–the–wind–blows."

And with those words the cock was gone.

Adam sat up in bed. Then he jumped
out and went to the window. The cock
was on the church steeple. Had he ever. . .?
It must have been a dream, but one of those
dreams so real it seemed to have happened.

There was a strange sound in the night—
a sound of stir and movement, the beat of
drums. The Bourbonnais were going and he
had not warned them!

He wondered about the time. The big
clock in the hall struck—he counted carefully—twelve.

It was too late for him to go out. His
mother. . . . But in wartime one did things
differently from peacetime. He could almost
hear the golden cock speaking. You must
decide for yourself. *I–tell–only–the–way–
the–wind–blows.*

Yes, in wartime, so his father had said,
a boy has to be a man. Adam hurried into

his clothes and crept downstairs. How that step creaked! Had they heard him? He listened a minute but there was no sound. He opened and closed the outside door gently. The night was dark.

He could find his way—he *had* to. Stumbling over stones that had not been there in the daytime, running when the ground was level and clear—wondering what lay in the shadows but not taking time to be afraid. . . .

He passed Paul's house. All the windows were dark, but that told nothing. If the harm was done, it was done. The soldiers were forming ranks. Would he see Pierre again? There were other things more important. He must find an officer.

Then suddenly—out of the darkness— Paul was beside him.

CHAPTER VI
AT THE CAMP

That put a different face on things.

"Paul," he said. *"What are you doing here?"*

"The same as you," Paul said. "I heard the stir in the camp. I heard the drums waking the men and I came out to see if I could talk to Pierre before he goes. Better watch out for snakes Adam, this field is full of them."

Now Adam knew he must not talk to Paul. That was the hardest of all, but it had to be done.

"I can't stay," he said quickly. "I have a message for—for one of the officers."

48   Paul looked at him sharply, then turned away. Adam went on toward the camp.

As luck had it, Pierre was on guard. Adam would not have to try to make himself understood by a soldier who did not speak his language.

"Pierre?" he said. Pierre looked at him in surprise. Adam rushed into his story, his words tumbling wildly over each other.

"A little slow," said Pierre. "I know English—but not when it gallops like a horse."

So Adam started all over again, holding his speech with a tight rein.

This time Pierre understood.

"Strawberries, fruit? Spies? Trust in us Adam, we do not sleep. We watch and we know. Your friend has not brought us any fruit. He has not talked to us."

"You think I was foolish?"

"I think you were brave to come here in the darkness, and wise to tell me."

"But suppose they know you are going?"

"Soon everyone will know. You cannot take a brigade out even at night without some people knowing."

Adam was not quite sure what to say next. Pierre smiled down at him.

"And that charming sister of yours. . . ."

"You mean Abigail?" Adam had never really noticed her charm. So many girls had pink cheeks and long fair hair. Didn't they?

"Of course I mean Abigail," Pierre said. "Please tell your sister that I will carry her in my heart as I go to fight."

Now Adam was really uncomfortable. How foolish could a soldier be? He blurted out, "Good-bye, Pierre," and was off.

Then he was angry with himself because he had not been polite. But imagine a soldier—a real soldier—being so silly about Abby! Oh, well. . . .

He went home through the darkness picking his way carefully once more. This time a burden seemed to have left him. He had done what seemed to be right. Perhaps he had imagined things—but Paul would never know. Possibly some day, when the war was all over, he would tell him, just to make things straight and clear? Perhaps his father would be home and they could talk things over? It was hard to be a boy and a man at the same time.

He reached the house and crept quietly up the stairs, taking a long stride over that creaking step. Back to his room and no one the wiser!

He lay in bed, thinking, but in a few minutes he was asleep. He did not hear the Bourbonnais and the Royal Deux Ponts go out.

Abigail did. "Good-bye, Pierre," she said to the darkness. "Come back, oh, *please* come back!"

There would be a new regiment coming in the next few days—the Saintonge and the Soissonais, new uniforms in different colors. There would be more artillery and their shining brass cannon; Pierre had said so. But nothing would be the same.

CHAPTER VII

THE BUTTON

Life most certainly was not the same. For two days there was the stir and movement of regiments arriving. The children still gathered around to watch, but these soldiers had little time to talk. Adam could not find one who spoke his language.

He tried what Abby had learned from Pierre.

"*Bon jour*," he said to a soldier.

"*Bon jour*," the soldier answered. And that was as far as they got. Adam tried it on others — and after that conversation stood still.

These regiments wore handsome uniforms, too. That soldier from the Saintonge, in white with red trimmings, Adam would have loved to talk with him. And the one from the Soissonais, in white and green, why *he* could only say "Good morning" and that again got them nowhere.

Almost before one knew it, they were gone. And again the days were all the same. The field was wide and green and empty, except for Adam and the sheep. There was no one to talk to but the golden cock, so far away on the steeple.

"*Bon jour*," said Adam. "*Bon jour*, cock." No answer came to his mind, perhaps the cock did not understand French.

One day, walking near the rock where Pierre had sat to talk, Adam stopped to

pick a few ripe strawberries. And there,
close to the rock, was a button!

Adam picked it up carefully, scarcely believing what he saw. It was a white button with the number 13 stamped on it. That was the number of Pierre's regiment— the number of the Bourbonnais! Adam had seen it on their buttons and on their big copper drums.

He held the button in his hand, wondering if it could be Pierre's. Maybe it was, maybe it wasn't. Still, it could be.

I hope it isn't his, Adam thought. What would Pierre do if a button were missing? What did soldiers do when buttons came off? Did the supply wagons carry buttons? There were so many things he wanted to know.

Of one thing he was sure; he would not let Abby get so much as a look at this button. She would want it, of course. Well, she wasn't going to have it, and that was that.

Adam put the button carefully in his pocket. He would keep it always, to remember those extraordinary days in his life. Some day he might show it to his children and say: "This is a French button. I was here when General Rochambeau's army came through." Some day, before that, he might even show it to Paul.

And some day the French troops might come back. Some day the war would be over. Some day his father would come home. . . . Adam scarcely dared to think of that.

CHAPTER VIII
THE FRENCH COME BACK

It was over a year later when the French army came marching back through Newtown. There had been news of a big battle fought at Yorktown—far down in Virginia. The French army and the French fleet had helped the Americans to win it.

But the war was not quite over. Adam's father had not yet come home. Adam was lonely. He longed for the real end of the war. Then—perhaps—he could be friends with Paul again.

It was good news that the French soldiers were coming. Would Pierre be with them? Perhaps he had been killed at Yorktown? 57

"Abby," Adam said, "they say that the French are near."

Abigail seemed only mildly interested.

"Perhaps Pierre will be with them," Adam went on.

Abby looked tall and very grown up. "What does that matter to me?" she asked. "You know that Seth and I are to be married when he comes back. And he will be back soon."

Adam was disgusted. Girls of Abby's age could be like that. They could forget so easily—and imagine Abby being old enough to have a house of her own! She was sixteen of course. . . . And Seth was not like Pierre. He didn't come from an exciting country across the ocean. He just lived next door!

Oh, well, he, Adam, would be there when the soldiers came. *He* would talk to

Pierre. Somehow in the last year he had
seldom talked to the golden cock. Now he
looked up at it and asked his old question.

"When will the soldiers come? Will
they come today?"

It was not that day, but the next. Adam
was there at the side of the road, and, by
some chance, Paul was beside him. Now
that the war was almost over could they be
friends again? Some day it would seem
easy to tell Paul about the strawberries. He
would understand.

They waited and waited. . . . Nothing
happened. Adam grew so tired that he
decided to show the button to Paul. He
took it out of his pocket.

"Of course they may want it," he said.
"Do you think so?"

There, at last, came the sound of horses'
hoofs. Rochambeau! The general and his

staff were coming by one road, the soldiers
by another.

Here they came! That man on the horse, the man who looked so important, was that Rochambeau? He had a kind face, but a mouth that looked as though it could be stern. Pierre had said that he had a temper. . . .

Adam leaned forward to keep the general in view as long as he could, to keep those few minutes in his mind for always. Now there would not be only a button to show. He could say, "I saw the great French general. I saw Rochambeau."

The staff had passed, riding into town. When the soldiers came, they would have to turn off the New York road, turn off to their camping ground. Without a word Adam and Paul went to the other road— and waited.

The sound of music came faintly, and again Adam's mind set words to it:

March, Papa Rochambeau,
March.

The gold and silver band came, marching through the leaves that were bright gold underfoot. A few yellow leaves came drifting down from the trees and settled on hats or shoulders. The men paid no attention to them, but marched with eyes straight ahead.

Now the soldiers began to come, their ranks flowing along like a white river. First came the Bourbonnais, their arms with the black cuffs on the sleeves swinging in time to the music. Their uniforms were not so white as they had been, but stained and worn.

There was Pierre! His arm and shoulder
were bandaged—he'd been wounded. Adam
leaned forward, but Pierre was looking
straight ahead. Then, could you believe it,
Abby was beside her brother—smiling,
waving. You never could tell what a girl
would do.

Pierre saw, out of the corner of his eye
he saw, without turning his head. The long
line of soldiers kept swinging off the main
road taking the turn to the camping ground.
Pierre swung with them.

There was a short, breathless silence.

"They couldn't want the button,
Adam," Paul said. "You must keep it."
Then, with sudden joy in his voice, "To-
morrow we'll see Pierre!"

Abby had gone back to the house, the
boys followed her. In his pocket Adam

64 kept his fingers tightly curled about the button, but he wasn't really thinking of it. He was thinking of something more important, hearing other words.

"Tomorrow we'll see Pierre."

It was the first time—for many, many months, that Paul had said "we."